陳明克 著譯
Poems and Translated by Chen Ming-Keh

詩帶著陽光

Poems With Sunshine

陳明克漢英雙語詩集
Mandarin-English

台灣詩叢 • Taiwan Poetry Series 22

【總序】詩推台灣印象

叢書策劃／李魁賢

　　進入21世紀，台灣詩人更積極走向國際，個人竭盡所能，在詩人朋友熱烈參與支持下，策畫出席過印度、蒙古、古巴、智利、緬甸、孟加拉、尼加拉瓜、馬其頓、秘魯、突尼西亞、越南、希臘、羅馬尼亞、墨西哥等國舉辦的國際詩歌節，並編輯《台灣心聲》等多種詩選在各國發行，使台灣詩人心聲透過作品傳佈國際間。

　　多年來進行國際詩交流活動最困擾的問題，莫如臨時編輯帶往國外交流的選集，大都應急處理，不但時間緊迫，且選用作品難免會有不周。因此，興起策畫【台灣詩叢】雙語詩系的念頭。若台灣詩人平常就有雙語詩集出版，隨時可以應用，詩作交流與詩人交誼雙管齊下，更具實際成效，對台灣詩的國際交流活動，當更加順利。

　　以【台灣】為名，著眼點當然有鑑於台灣文學在國際間名目不彰，台灣詩人能夠有機會在國際努力開拓空間，非為個人建立知名度，而是為推展台灣意象的整體事功，期待開創台灣文學的長久景象，才能奠定寶貴的歷史意義，台灣文學終必在世界文壇上佔有地位。

　　實際經驗也明顯印證，台灣詩人參與國際詩交流活動，很受重視，帶出去的詩選集也深受歡迎，從近年外國詩人和出版社與本人合作編譯台灣詩選，甚至主動翻譯本人詩集在各國文學雜誌或詩刊發表，進而出版外譯詩集的情況，大為增多，即可充分證明。

　　承蒙秀威資訊科技公司一本支援詩集出版初衷，慨然接受【台灣詩叢】列入編輯計畫，對台灣詩的國際交流，提供推進力量，希望能有更多各種不同外語的雙語詩集出版，形成進軍國際的集結基地。

【序】

　　這本選集包括五十八首詩及其英譯。其中2015年至2023年的詩有五十三首，2015年以前的詩已選入2019出版的漢英詩集：《船塢裡》（*In Dock*），因此只選五首。這五十八首詩，仍是作者堅持的，對人性的反省、探討，從人在現實生活所受的考驗，尋找生命價值並實現生命價值、追求生命昇華的過程。如短詩，〈落花〉、〈雨〉等；如情詩，〈海芋都是妳〉、〈黃絲巾〉等；如哲理詩〈瓶中花〉、〈流水〉、〈日影〉等；而更加入世的，如〈人〉、〈雞〉等；又如從〈隔離〉，2003年SARS短暫流行，2019年底疑似SARS再起。〈踏春〉，2020確定是COVID-19，直到2023的〈詩帶著陽光〉，20年斷續在瘟疫陰影中。也因近年的戰爭，而有〈驚慌的麻雀〉、〈搶奪春天〉等。可說是一本既深入內心，也凝視外在的選集。

目次

夢

我好像還在
微風中的樹影下走著
不時期待地
望著樹後

很奇怪地我在
黃土場中奔跑
雲柱在附近漸漸生成
我一圈一圈原地繞著
有些模糊的人影
沉默地走著
我又得再一次轉彎
（雲柱好像旋轉了起來）

眼前忽然錯落枯萎的木麻黃
風呼嘯地把樹木折彎
恍若吹著口哨的風

好像捆住我
我穿行於搖晃的樹林中
沒有任何期望

她卻忽然走來
（雖然背著光）
似笑非笑地擦身而過
我看著她溶入雲霧的背影
苦苦思索
（沒有風
沒有木麻黃
沒有黃土操場）

1998/1

隔離

陽光悄悄進入房間
我好像聽到陽光的腳步聲
我迷茫的被光芒浮起來
不能控制地飄飛
卻突然看到掉在枕邊的口罩
我慌張地伸手
才驚醒過來

客廳裡我小一的小孩
蹲伏地板上
以積木堆好城鎮河流丘陵
他漸漸張開雙臂
輕輕拍著
在積木中哼著歌飛翔
如陽台悠遊的蝴蝶

我嚴肅地要他戴口罩
他說他無法飛翔
喘著氣跌坐地上
碰倒他的積木世界
嘩嘩的聲音令我心煩
我不禁地吼叫

他流下眼淚手臂垂放
如戴著口罩的蝴蝶
失去飛翔的天賦
從花朵中摔落

2003/5/9
SARS 流行中

新葉

工人掃著菩提樹落葉
飛起的塵沙中
陽光閃耀
我忽然相信
會有一樁我長久等待的
神奇的改變

她悄悄走來
拖著我走的時空因此震裂
我一腳跨出缺口
痴痴看著她甜美地笑

菩提樹也因為她來？
突然枯黃　葉子劇烈地掉落
重生一般換了新葉

她在樹影中　漸漸走遠
我呆呆望著
一再壓抑奔向她的熱望
唉！人不能更換新葉

2004/5/23

螢火蟲之湖

我年輕時曾經嘲笑
孤單的螢火蟲
從久停的湖邊草叢
飛向湖面
繞著水中搖晃的光點

我夢見早已忘掉的
小學上學途中
嘻笑奔跳的同伴
我在笑起來時驚醒
急忙要畫下他們
卻已模糊渙散

螢火蟲！我們來交換
只有人才能擁有的夢
遠遠不如你的湖水

2004/8/28

春夜

深夜風忽然轉向
春雨遲疑地跟隨
終於綿密地敲打窗戶
青蛙一隻隻醒過來
試著輕輕鳴叫

牠們看到泡沫
從窗戶不斷冒出
那是人的夢
像水花即開即謝

蛙鳴時漲大的氣囊
卻從不爆裂
牠們放膽高聲歡唱

2006/4/22

秋風（一）

台灣欒樹喜悠悠
開著小黃花

秋風蕩來蕩去
不經意經過

為早已滿地的落花
被罵得無處躲藏

好無辜啊
又撞得花掉落

2015/9/24

海芋都是妳

遠遠看到潔白的海芋
像穿著白衣的少女
怯怯地等誰？

年少的我們無知？
離別時都還燦爛地笑著
心裡面微微的酸疼
阻擋不了未來
夢一般的引誘

妳穿著一襲白衣
春風繞著妳
輕輕拉妳的衣裙

我們都失神地聽
風中隱藏的祕密

但現在最怕想起
輕率地放開妳的手
妳被人群一下子淹沒
只看到人影晃動
看不見妳

一株株海芋輕輕搖晃
像走動的人群
我轉身急急走避
微風中卻有妳的聲音

「是我啊
我仍穿著白衣
怕你找不到
整片都是我
沒有人能再遮住我」

瓶中花

幾道陽光從窗戶
斜斜進來
照著花瓶
花還做著夢
追著風跳舞

突然被拔出來
丟進垃圾桶
花為失去花瓶
哭泣　花瓣掉落
感覺到死亡

它們還是不相信
「曾在泥土中
生長開花
拉著風跳舞」
那朵被嘲笑至死的
花不肯停地說的

它還在說
這是不死不活

2015/12/27

秋風（二）

秋風點燃楓葉
卻又後悔
極力要火慢慢地燒

竟然帶著楓葉
在天空跳舞

真希望我是
秋風所造

2016/10/10

秋夜之雨

秋天的深夜
誰遠遠地走過來？
窗外輕輕徘徊

呢喃對我？
說什麼

喔，只是雨

是我凝望的
夕陽暈染的雲？
來回應我

2016/11/10

樹下老人

吹落枯葉
樹會長出嫩葉
重生

樹下老人等待
秋風跳下來
吹落他的白髮

2016/12/9

盛開之櫻

石雕的少女
是永恆不滅的吧

搖晃的樹影中
為什麼痴痴望著
短暫的燦爛的櫻花

我摘下一朵櫻花
卻無法插在
她的頭髮

2017/4/5
名古屋中央公園 TV tower 附近

人

這次
操偶者猛拉著線
木偶就是不動

拉扯著　線斷了
木偶向後跌倒

操偶者轉頭
如巫師巫婆
咬牙詛咒
尋找其它木偶

嗯，操偶者是人

那木偶卻突然站起來
握拳瞪視
撲向操偶者

啊！它是人

2017/9/10
《笠》322期 2017/12
入選《2017台灣現代詩選》

一日之花

深愛陽光的花
為什麼匆匆掉落

唉──追著太陽

2017/11/22

春風

蝴蝶是被春風
誘拐的花

緊追著風
要拉住風飛舞

深秋風變了
蝴蝶跌落雜草中
再也回不去

2017/12/7

落花

一朵疊一朵
飄落地上的櫻花

「不要哭
現在能緊牽著手
不再怕被打散」

2018/2/27

一個人的等待

灰茫的出海口
一個人在沙洲等待
不靠岸的船

2018/10/29
9/24 清晨眺望淡水河口

心事

苦苓樹下
到了夜晚花香
更加濃郁飄漾

但會被花香吸引的
蜜蜂蝴蝶都
已入眠啊

是心事
是密密麻麻的花
說不出的心事

2019/3/21

小草

寂寞的小草
再怎麼努力
還是埋沒在
幽深的草堆裡

它不知道
它等待的是什麼
也不知道
露珠已掛在草尖

誰天天
為它戴上？

2019/3/30

流水

流水中流著的樹葉
知道流水
知道會沉沒

我感覺它們
在哭在笑
它們對流水
時而柔聲耳語
時而掙扎著
想駕馭水流

但流水
不知道有樹葉
也不知道
自己不停流著

我知道
時間也是這樣

2019/8/9
《笠》338期2020/10

關渡之秋

秋天
候鳥還沒來
關渡溼地靜得
只有落葉
掉在木棧道

欒樹花剛盛開
我輕輕走進
樹下幽幽的小路

我聽到她
像隻小貓躲在
我背後
踮著腳迂迴走近
細碎的腳步聲
忽有忽無

我想著怎樣才能
回身抓住她
啊！靠近了
我緩緩倒退
突然轉身

她撲進我的懷裡
卻化成欒樹落花
從我身上
滑落到地面

2019/10/8

滿月之花

滿月升起時
油菜花痴痴望著

彷彿知道
一生僅有一次

2020/1/10

踏春

瘟疫渡海了？

沒人來的稻田裡
盛開的波斯菊
沮喪地等待著

一直到黃昏
才驚喜地看到
花海中一群人
忽隱忽現

波斯菊激動得搖晃
要更靠近
那群人

忽然跳起來
飛起來
啊！麻雀！一群！

2020/1/29

落葉（一）

落葉的樹下
她抬頭尋找誰

風吹散她腳邊
一片落葉的嘆息

2020/2/8

擁抱

木棉花
一朵接一朵掉落
都望著人
走過去

風中落葉
跌跌撞撞過來
擁抱花

2020/4/10

夕陽和花

望著花的夕陽
竟急著要偏向
要遠離

他發覺那朵花
正望著他

花為他的害羞高興
她不知道
他必須孤獨

2020/4/13

愛上太陽的露珠

愛上夕陽的露珠
漫長的黑夜中
獨自在草葉
無聲哭泣

朝陽升起時
它驚喜呼喚
「這裡！我在這裡！
是我啊！」

陽光飛奔過來
它卻突然消失

2020/4/20

大災變

瘟疫病毒
從潘朵拉的盒子飛出
還拉著什麼出來？
撞破窗玻璃
警衛躲在角落發抖

會是大災殃？

這些都被掩蓋
只當是野味惹的小事

大地還不知道
就變暗了
深紅的晚霞是
天空流出的血
人開始一個接一個
覺得鼻孔被堵住

但那是誰
仍然為稻草
撒下露珠

2020/4/26

瘟疫中

隔離後　他日漸
喜歡坐到窗邊
他愛戀的陽光城市
如今人和一棟棟大樓
經常浸泡在薄霧中
他等不到有人抬頭看他

隔離的第七天
城市在霧中消失
他叫喊　只引來回音
人遺棄他逃出城

陽光抱著露珠落向他
他覺得他死於瘟疫了
珍卻從露珠走出來
在樓下急切呼喚他

他跑到陽台邊
好多人揮手喊著
「一起！我們一起對抗病毒」

沒人拋棄他，沒人逃出城
珍含淚揚著玫瑰
柔聲叫著他的名字

2020/5/13
《笠》342期 2021/04

海的夢

密布的烏雲縫隙
陽光斜斜落向
熟睡的海

海天相接處
一道光
忽亮忽暗

海眨著眼睛啊

匯集眾水的海
竟夢見
它是一顆露珠
飄落到草尖

所有動植物
也都夢見海的夢
難怪牠們沒有戰爭

做為人的我
卻夢見從草尖的露珠
站起來　張望
還有誰？

2020/6/2
《自由副刊》2022/4/14

被拔掉的舌頭

在荒野奔走
突然驚醒
覺得被換了舌頭

外來者議員指著
我們首次選出的官員
嘲笑：「什麼不三不四說的
還為他們創造文字」

那假舌一動就痛
我還在少年起
糾纏至今的惡夢中？

八、九歲的我走進教室
被高大的老師抓住
撬開嘴拔掉舌頭
我摀著流血的嘴巴
父母聽不懂我說什麼

我不懂怎會有這惡夢？
在荒野奔跑尋找

那群外來者代表
嘩然叫喊刪掉台語預算
「用它燒掉他們拔掉的舌頭」

他們在我背後追著
我要趕快在荒野找到
被拔掉的舌頭

2020/6/7

海浪

奔向沙灘
他看到她微笑
伸出手等他

什麼樣的力量
剎那間反轉
猛猛拉著他
奔回大海

他一直望著沙灘
那男子踏著
薄薄一層水
走向她

他拉住她的手？
遠去的海浪又回來

2020/6/1

風

吹動花的風
看著搖曳的花姿
滿足地微笑

誰像風看著我？

啊！花飄落

2020/6/9

驚慌的麻雀

黃昏稻田裡
隱身稻叢深處的麻雀
一大群驚慌飛起

不是準備過夜？
又一大群
無預兆竄飛起來

不曾有感覺
現在我卻流淚
滴落先人數百年來
居住的土地

從沒踏足這裡的
那個國一直宣稱
是她的地
軍機軍艦一直圍繞進逼

麻雀飛遠了
不是麻雀的我
飛不起來

2020/6/9

夕陽

今天不看了
夕陽之美是幻象

卻不時偷偷瞄一下

被飛落細草的
小鳥發現

輕聲對我叫
夕陽從雲縫
出來了

2020/6/12

孤單的人

不會有人的
高架鐵軌
那人孤單走著

他等待的雲
會在哪裡下來？

2020/6/15

落葉（二）

陰暗的山徑
垂死的落葉
不知被雨打落
在祈求的陽光中醒來

它看不見同伴
它呼喚著

2020/7/26

雨

雨聲不間斷
花終於掉落

雨怎樣說動了花？

2021/2/11

月蝕

第一次看月全蝕
那時是少年的他

第一次有個少女
在耳邊柔聲說
「下一次月蝕
我們會在哪裡？」

他不記得那時
為什麼急著想知道
怎麼預測
下一次月蝕
是什麼時候

她好像突然消失
融入黑夜

多年後他看著
又即將復圓的月
彷彿聽見她
仍然輕柔地說
「你找到我了？」

「妳在哪裡？」
他焦急轉動身體
「歷經這麼多折磨
妳怎找得到我？」

只有一朵
正在開的玫瑰花
從枯葉中

2021/6/22

淡水落日

夕陽從雲裡出來
紅著臉

那輪船停下來
等著它

如果船接住它
我們會在永恆中

「如果船進入夕陽
會到另一個
全新的美麗世界」

「你要拉著我跑過去」
「我會為妳摘一朵花」

我們卻看著
夕陽被海面上的雲
咬碎吞下

2021/9/22

詩的盛會

螢幕中的詩人
朗誦著詩

坐在椅子的詩人
想著　有時回頭看
他們陳列的詩集
默默吟誦

瘟疫還追著時間
追著人
又抓到了誰？

現在誰在吟詩？
啊！一首又一首
圖書館關門後

瘟疫抓不到詩

2022/9/20
2022 福爾摩莎詩歌節開幕式
淡江大學圖書館

晚霞

是晚霞還是彩帶？
輕輕飄向將捷
　彷彿潔白的宮殿
為了尋找她

卻不知
要落到哪裡？

難道她躲進
小丘綠草裡面
望著彩帶微笑？

2022/9/19

水滴

一顆又一顆
鋼珠般的水滴
掉落黃昏的水池

怎會沒有水花？
也不沉沒？

哎呀！是落在
天空中的晚霞

2022/9/21

爬到頂端的人

天空的晚霞
快消失了

快步爬到
步道頂端的人
只要往上一躍
就可以跳到晚霞

為眾人控訴
發動侵略戰爭
瘋狂想要
奴役他人的人魔

卻望著地面
想聽清楚
人魔要給他什麼？

晚霞又在
無聲的嘆息中
消散

2022/9/23

不時花

淡水河邊
那棵鳳凰木
還稀稀疏疏
開著紅花

是不時花啊
竟望著觀音山
不斷默默祈禱

不時花就不時花
還能祈求什麼？

白茫茫的雲氣
突然變得橘紅
飛向觀音山
跳進河裡
踏水奔向鳳凰花

那不時花啊

2022/9/20

蔓藤與詩

寫了詩的陶葉
貼在忠寮
鄉路邊駁崁
不再枯萎

人邊走
邊輕輕唸著詩

啊！蔓藤
爬進陶葉裡面
唸詩擁抱詩

「我不要枯萎
我要化為陶葉
化為詩」

寫了詩的人
長青不老？

2022/10/12

搶奪春天

春天是誰的？

俄羅斯的戰車
侵入烏克蘭
輾碎春田
為搶奪春天

那個人揉著眼睛
注視著
觀察怎樣入侵
能奪取台灣之春

我經過春田
低頭啄食的水鳥
突然奔竄
激起一行行水花
牠們嬉戲？驅逐？

一下子就停下來
各自遠遠站著
哪一隻水鳥
能搶到春天？
獨佔春天？

2023/2/26

雞

學生問
為什麼那個人
會大聲叫嚷
要回中國祭祖

「是衣錦還鄉？」
「是告老還鄉？」
他們不斷爭論

我清咳幾聲說起
小時候我家
放牧的一些雞
起初我很厭惡
被叫去，趕雞回來過夜
雞四處亂跑
不知要追那一隻

有次看到隔壁阿姨
撮口叫著：「珠～珠」
雞一隻隻冒出來
奔向她　邊啄米粒
邊走進雞舍

「別家的雞也跑向她？」

「不！不！只有她養的
平常她就這樣叫
這樣餵牠們」

甚至想殺雞來吃
也是這樣叫
牠們也一樣
飛奔回來

「老師！這是寓言嗎？」
「難道那個人
是中國養的雞！？」
「啊！雞是牲畜啊！」
學生又喧嘩起來

2023/3/21

愛之美

愛，美如
花瓣上的露珠

幾時花卻飄零？
露珠落地無影？

喔！又開了一朵花

從哪裡來的？

2023/3/28

永遠

新造的
磚砌月牙門洞
他們牽著手
不知望著什麼
喃喃說永遠

弦月又一次
進入門洞內
來找那對情人
只看到不相關的我

我輕撫
百年門柱之磚
忽然聽到誰對我
溫柔地輕聲說
「不是說永遠？」

2023/9/21
淡水紅樓

盡頭

又忍不住
匆匆離開人群
尋找夕陽

又要急切地問？
為什麼要夕陽
爆裂焚燒
在空中飛散

不！我只驚覺
已不再激盪
給我的
不過是這麼多

誰在我背後嘆息？
我看見她
宛如星星的眼睛

凝視我走向我
卻忽然看不見

「你還沒找到
我造的你」

2023/9/23

百年之瓦

不要碰觸它
時間被它抓住了
會跑出來拖走你

2023/9/24
淡水忠寮

日影

初秋的樹下
她是日影
輕靈如微風

和她共舞的日影
忽然凝結成落葉

她繞著那落葉
想翻開它
一直喃喃地問
「為什麼要躲到
落葉下」

落葉被風吹走
葉片下的日影
去哪裡了？

2023/9/25

詩帶著陽光

他們被什麼困住？
無法過來

忠寮彎彎的小路
溪邊的駁崁
他們的詩怎會寫在
芋葉化成的陶葉
等待他們

只要他們唸出詩
瘟疫的魔咒
就是陽光下的冰雹

我在斑駁的陽光
小路中彎來彎去
終於
找到他們的詩

誰在朗頌他們的詩？
他們回頭微笑
詩帶著陽光過來
邊跑邊跳

不再有
永遠不再有瘟疫、戰爭

2023/10/8

風中草

兩枝草快牽住手
忽然被風吹散

它們又
在風中靠近
急著想說什麼

風是怎麼啦
又吹散它們

一對情侶忙著
推近這兩枝草
風卻一再繞過
他們的手掌
分開草

風越來越大
他們突然被吹得
跌坐草地

他們緊緊牽著手
茫然像兩枝草

2023/10/31

黃絲巾

風似有若無
綠樹下她圍著
黃絲巾？
遠遠的過來

我仍是個少年
拿著剛寫成的詩
凝望著她
走向前又退後

她撥開頭髮
和飄起來的絲巾
看到我
絲巾忽被風吹走

我追著絲巾
深黃的葉子
紛紛飛向我
我忽然是個老人

她不見了
絲巾飄向哪裡？
校門裡追著笑聲
少男少女跑出來

2023/10/31

風鈴木

塵霾中
風鈴花歡歡喜喜
一下子盛開

一下子飄零散落

唉！如此塵世
不如早逝吧

又為什麼急著
長滿密麻麻的綠葉
盼望明年？

2024/3/23

一隻螢火蟲

一、

天快黑時，他注視
流經他的地的水流
散落塑膠碗、袋子，瓶罐
他喃喃自語，一改為建地就賣

一隻螢火蟲卻在水邊
閃爍著　飛向他
繞著他忽前忽後
他好奇地跟過去

他看到一個老人和淑女
費力撈出水中垃圾

那淑女想挑起兩擔垃圾
他急忙搶過來

她偏頭淺笑
望著喘吁吁的他

螢火蟲照亮她眼睛

二、

他們來回幾趟後
螢火蟲從哪飛出來？
像不停的煙火
分不出是溪流
還是螢河

她鈴鐺般笑出聲
「阿公！辦到了！」
那老人回身對他彎腰
忽跳入光點閃爍的溪流
他驚叫、衝過去
她跑向他，拉住他

那老人從飛舞的光點
站起來　是個小孩
向我們揮手
一再回頭終於走遠

她幽幽說：「謝謝你！
阿公重生了」

三、

「那淑女呢？」

他長長嘆口氣：「我收回地
清垃圾、不用農藥、化肥
只用大地給的」

「哇！又長又寬
流動搖漾的螢河！」

他默默在螢河邊徘徊
他在找誰？

2024/4/22

作者簡介

陳明克

1986年於清華大學獲得物理博士學位。1987年，加入笠詩社。現在是笠詩社社務委員。結集的詩集有十二本，中短篇小說集有兩本。獲得九項文學獎。作品探索生命的意義。常以隱喻表現。

英語篇

Poems With Sunshine

Preface

  This anthology includes fifty-eight poems and their English translations. Among them, there are fifty-three poems from 2015 to 2023. The poems before 2015 have been selected into the Mandarin-English poetry collection published in 2019: In Dock, so only five poems were selected. These fifty-eight poems are still the author's insistence on introspection and probe of human nature, the process of finding and realizing the value of life and pursuing the sublimation of life based on the tests people face in real life. Such as short poems, "Falling Flowers", "Rain", etc.; such as love poems, "All of Calla Lilies Are You", "The Yellow Scarf", etc.; such as philosophical poems, "Flowers in the Vase", "Flowing Water", "The Images of Sun Through Leaves", etc.; And going more into the society, such as "Human", "Chicken", etc.; and the poem, "Isolation", was written when SARS was briefly spreading in 2003, and SARS was suspected of resurrecting at the end of 2019. "Hiking in Spring" was written when it was determined to be COVID-19 in 2020, and until 2023 the poem, "Poems With Sunshine" was written, it has been in the shadow of the plague intermittently for 20 years. Also due to the wars in recent years, there are "The Frightened Sparrows", "Robbing the Spring", etc. It can be said to be an anthology that both goes deep into the heart and gazes at the outside.

CONTENTS

A Dream

I seemed to still walk
In the shadows of trees, blew by breezes
From time to time, I expected and
Looked behind trees

Strangely, I was
Running in a yellow-earthed field
Pillars of clouds were growing up gradually
I revolved round the field over and over again
Some blurred shadows with human shape
Walked silently
I had to make a turn again
(pillars of clouds seemed to start to revolve)

I suddenly saw faded beef woods were interlaced
The wind raved and bent the branches
The wind, whistled as humane did

Seemed to sheave me

I was passing through the trees

With no hope

But unexpectedly, she came to me

(Although light fell from her back)

she brushed past me with an unclear smile

I looked her melting into clouds and fogs

I reasoned it with hard effort

(I found no wind

no beefwoods

no yellow-earthed field)

1998/1

Isolation

Sunshine entered my room quietly
I seemed to hear the footsteps of sunshine
I was floating up in sunshine in confusion
drifting uncontrollably
But suddenly, I saw the mask, left around my pillow
I stretched out my hand in surprise
And waked up

In the sitting room, my ten-year old kid
squatted and prostrated on the ground
He built towns, rivers and hills by building blocks
He opened his hands
and flapped them as wings
He hummed and flied among wooden blocks
as butterflies, playing leisurely in the balcony

I seriously asked him to wear mask

He said he could not fly if he put on mask

He panted and fell down on the ground

knocking down his world of wooden blocks

The voice of falling blocks made me fidgety

I could not repress yells

He shed tears and put down hands feebly

as a butterfly, wearing a mask

losing the born gift of flying

fell down from flowers

2003/5/9

(in the epidemic days of SARS)

New Leaves

Workers are sweeping the fallen leaves of bodhi trees

In the flying dusts

Sunshine is shining

I suddenly believe

A mysterious change, I have waited for a long time,

Will happen

She comes silently

The space-time, dragging me to go, is shaken to break

I step one of my feet out from the breach

Besotted to look at her sweet smile

Is it also because of her coming?

The leaves of bodhi trees became dry and yellow suddenly, fell
    violently

Bodhi trees grow new leaves, as they are reborn

She is in the shadows of trees, going farther and farther

I watch her intently

once and again, suppressing my desire of running to her

Oy! Human cannot grow new leaves to change

2004/5/23

Glowworm's Lake

When I was young, I ever sneered at

A lonely glowworm

From the grasses, it stayed for a long while, near the lake

It flew to the lake

Encircled the swaying dribbles of light in water

I dreamed of what I had forgotten since a long time ago

On the way to the primary school

My friends ran, jumped and cackled

I waked up when I burst out laughing

I hurriedly intended to draw them

But they were blurred and dispersed

Glowworm! Let's exchange

Dreams, which only human can have

Are so incomparable to your lake

2004/8/28

Spring Night

The wind suddenly changes direction at night
The spring rain follows hesitatingly
Finally knock on the window continuously
The frogs wake up one by one
Tring to pipe gently

They see water foams
Rising from the window constantly
Those are human's dreams
As flowers bloom and fade soon

The airbags of frogs are inflated when they croak
But never burst
They sing loudly, boldly and with confidence

2006/4/22

The Autumn Breeze

Taiwan flame-gold trees
are so happy to be in
yellow blossoms

The autumn breeze, hanged around
and came by the way,

For the fallen flowers everywhere on the ground
the breeze is so blamed
that it has nowhere to hide

How innocent!
But now
it bumps the flowers to fall

2015/9/24

All of Calla Lilies Are You

The white calla lilies from a distance

Look like a girl in white

Whom are you waiting timidly for?

Were we ignorant when we were young?

We were all smiling brightly when we parted

The slight ache in my heart

Couldn't stop me from being tempted

To the dreamlike future

You were wearing in white

The spring breeze surrounded you

Gently pulled your skirt

We all listened absentmindedly

The secrets hidden in the breeze

But now I'm most afraid to remind of
I let go of your hand flippantly
You were suddenly masked by the crowd
I only saw contours shaking
Without you

The calla lilies sway gently
As if a moving crowd
I turn around and hurry away
But there is your voice in the breeze

"It's me
I still wear in white
I'm afraid you can't find me
The whole sea of flowers is me
No one can cover me anymore"

Flowers in The Vase

From the window, a few rays of sunlight

Come in at a tilt

shine on the vase

All flowers are still dreaming

Dancing after the wind

They are suddenly pulled out

thrown in a trash can

Petals falling, they cry

for they lose the vase

They feel the death

They still don't believe that

"Being in the dirt

We ever grew, bloomed and Pulled the wind to dance with"

One of them said again and again,

which they laughed at until they die

That flower is still saying

"In vase. we are neither dead nor alive"

2015/12/27

Autumn Wind

Autumn wind in fall ignite maple leaves
But soon, it regretfully
tried to burn the leaves
More slowly

It even embraced maple leaves
To dance in the sky

I really wished I was
made by the autumn wind

2016/10/10

Rain in Fall Night

In the deep night of fall
Who comes from far away
And wanders softly
outside the window

What does she whisper to me?

Oh! It is only rain

Is it the sunset cloud,
which I stared at
Comes to respond to me?

2016/11/10

An Old Man Under the Trees

If the withered leaves
are blown down
Trees will grow tender leaves
And will be reborn

An old man under the trees
waited for the wind of autumn
to jump down and blow down
his white hair

2016/12/9

Blooming Cherries

The young lady, a stone carving
Must be eternal

In the wavering shadows
Why does she infatuatedly look at
Cherry blossoms,
short and resplendent

I pick a cherry blossom
But can't stick into her hairs

2017/4/5
Near TV tower in Central Park, Nagoya

A Person

This time
The puppeteer tugs at the string
The puppet just won't move

As they pull at each other, the thread is broken
The puppet falls backwards

The puppeteer turns his head
like a wizard
He grits his teeth, curses
And finds other puppets

Well, the puppeteer is a person

The puppet suddenly stands up,

Clenches its fists and stares

And pounces on the puppeteer

Ah! It is a person

2017/9/10

One-day Flowers

They love sunshine deeply
But fall down hurriedly

Oy! They pursue the sun

2017/11/22

Spring Breezes

Butterflies are flowers
Abducted by spring breezes

Holding breezes in arms
They fly and dance

The breezes have changed in deep fall
Coming back no more
Butterflies fall to wild grasses

2017/12/7

Falling Flowers

One by one, cherry blossoms
are falling on the ground

"Do not cry
Now we can tightly hold each other
No longer afraid of being broken up"

2018/2/27

One's Waiting

It is grey in estuary

At sandbar, one is waiting for

A ship, not sailing to the shore

2018/10/29
Looking at Tamsui River Estuary
in the early morning on September 24,2018.

Something in Heart

Under bitter berry trees
At spring night, the scent of flowers
Is richer and swaying

But, the bees and butterflies
Which could be attracted
Have fallen asleep

Oh! It is something in heart
The dense flowers can not
Speak out

2019/3/21

A Little Grass

A lonely little grass
Is still buried in
Dark and deep grasses
No matter how hard it tries

It doesn't know
What it waits for?
Nor it knows
Dewdrops have been hung on its tip

Who wears a dewdrop for it
Every day?

2019/3/30

Running Water

Leaves flowing in the running water
are aware of running water
and that they will sink

I feel them
crying and laughing
Facing the running water, they
sometimes whisper softly
sometimes struggle
trying to control the current

But running water.
does not know there are leaves
does not know either
it keeps flowing

I know

So is time

2019/8/9

The Fall of Guandu

In fall
migratory birds have not come yet
Guandu wetland is so quiet that
only leaves are
falling on the boardwalk

Flowers of Taiwan gold-rain trees
are just in full bloom
I walk gently into
a secluded path under the trees

I hear her
like a kitten hiding behind me
She walks on tip toes to and fro
The finely divided footsteps
suddenly appear and disappear

I think about how to
go back and grab her
Ah! She is coming closer
I am slowly going backwards
and suddenly turn back

She runs into my arms
but turns into the little flowers
that fall on me
slide from me to the ground

2019/10/8

Cauliflowers

Watching the rising full moon

Cauliflowers are looking at it obsessively

As if they know

It is only once in their life

2020/1/10

Hiking in Spring

Have the plagues crossed the sea?

No visitor appears in the rice field, harvested
Blooming cosmos flowers in waiting
are depressed

Until dusk, they do not find
a group of people flicker
in surprise
in the sea of flowers

The flowers are so excited
as to sway and lean closer
the crowd

Suddenly they jump up

and soon fly

Ah! sparrows! a group!

2020/1/29

Fallen Leaves

Under the trees, leaves are dropping
Whom does she look up to find?

The sigh of a leaf,
fallen around her feet,
is blown off by the wind

2020/2/8

Embrace

Flowers of kapok trees

Drop one by one

They all look at people

Who walk across

In the wind, fallen leaves

Run and fall down

To hug flowers

2020/4/10

Sunset and a Flower

Sunset, staring at a flower
leans away
and goes away eagerly

It finds, that flower
Is looking at him intently

That flower is happy for it blushes
But not aware
It must be lonely

2020/4/13

A Dewdrop in Love

A Dewdrop, falling in love with the sunset

Cries silently

Alone in the blade of grass

In the long night

When the sun rises

"Here! I am here!

It's me!"

It calls in surprise

To the dewdrop,

The sun runs and flies

The dewdrop suddenly disappears

2020/4/20

Cataclysm

Plague virus
Flied out of Pandora's Box
What else did they pull out?
They hit and broke the window glass
The guards shivered in the corners

Will it be a disaster?

They are all covered up
Regarding as a little trouble induced by eating wild animals

Before the earth knew it
It was getting dark
Crimson sunset clouds
Are blood from the sky's wounds
One by one, people start to
Feel nostrils blocked

But who is he

Still dropping the dews

For rice straws

2020/4/26

In The Plague

In home quarantine,
he likes more and more
to sit beside the window
The city, he loved, was full of sunshine
Now people and buildings are often
soaked in mist row by row
He waits but none looks up at him

The seventh day in quarantine
The city disappears in the fog
He yells but none responds except echoes
People fled the city and left him alone

Sunlight holding dews falls upon him
He thinks he died of the plague
But Jane comes out from a dewdrop
Calling him urgently downstairs

147

He runs to the balcony and looks down

Many people shout and wave

"Together! Let's fight against the virus together"

None fled the city, none abandoned him

Jane waves roses in tears

and softly calls his name

2020/5/13

The Sea is Dreaming

From the gaps of dense clouds
the slanted sunlight falls
upon the sleeping sea

Where the sea meets the sky
a beam of light is flickering

Oh! The sea blinks its eyes

The sea has gathered so much water
but dreams
it is a dewdrop
falling to the tip of a grass

All animals and plants
Also dream the sea's dream
No wonder no war is amongst them

But I, a human being

Dream I stand up from a dewdrop

On the tip of a grass

And look around

Whom else I can find

2020/6/2

Tongue Being Pulled Out

I am running in the wilderness
Suddenly I wake up
I feel like my tongue has been exchanged

Legislators of outsiders are pointing at
The officials, we elected for the first time
Ridicule: "How rude they speak
Why create words, used to write, for them?"

I feel pain when I move the fake tongue
Am I still in the nightmare
Entangled me since my teenage?

At the age of eight or nine, I walked into the classroom
Caught by a tall teacher in black
He Pried my mouth and extracted my tongue
I covered my bleeding mouth
Parents didn't understand what I am saying

I don't understand how this nightmare can happen
What do I find in running in the wilderness?

The group of outsiders
Shout to delete Taiwanese budget
"Use it to burn out their tongues, being extracted"

They chase behind me
I must quickly find my extracted tongue, which has casually thrown
    away in the wilderness

2020/6/7

Sea Wave

Running towards the beach
he sees she smiles
waits for him and
reaches out her hand

What kind of power
instantly reversed
pulls him violently
to run back to the sea

He keeps looking at the beach
That man is stepping on
a thin layer of water
walks to her

Does he hold her hand?

The wave which has gone away

comes back

2020/6/1

The Breeze

The breeze which blows and
looks at the flowers swaying,
smiles contentedly

Who looks at me like the breeze?

Ah! Flowers fall in the breeze

2020/6/9

The Frightened Sparrows

At dusk, a large group of sparrows,

hidden in deep rice grasses

are frightened to fly out

Aren't they ready to stay overnight?

Another big group of sparrows

Wildly fly out without any omen

I never paid attention to them

But now I shed tears

Dripping on the land , on which ancestors

have lived for hundreds of years

That country never set foot here

But always claims, our land is her land

Military aircraft and warships have surrounded

to press us over and over

Sparrows have flew away

I am not a sparrow

I can't fly

2020/6/9

Sunset

I don't watch the sunset today
Its beauty is an illusion

But I secretly take a look at times

I was found by a small bird
Which flied down on the tiny grass

It whispers to me
From the cloud gap
Sunset is coming out

2020/6/12

The Lonely One

A man walks alone on
the elevated railroad track,
which no one will walk on

Where will the cloud be?
Does he wait for it comes down?

2020/6/15

A Fallen Leaf

On the dark hill trail
a dying leaf doesn't know
it was beaten down by the rain
It wakes up in the sunshine, it prayed

It can't find its friends
It is calling

2020/7/26

Rain

Rain sounds nonstop
Flowers finally fall

How did rain persuade flowers to fall?

2021/2/11

Lunar Eclipse

The first time he watched the lunar eclipse

He was a teenager

It was also the first time a girl

Said softly in his ears

"At the next lunar eclipse

where will we be?"

He doesn't remember

At that time

why he was so anxious to know

how to predict

when the next lunar eclipse

would be

It seemed she disappeared suddenly

And blended into the night

Years later he looks at
the next lunar eclipse
The moon is about to be full again
He seems to hear her
Still speaking softly
"You found me?"

"Where are you?"
He turns around anxiously
"After so many tortures
how can you find me?"

Only a rose is blooming
In dead leaves

2021/6/22

Sunset at Tamsui Estuary

The sunset comes out from clouds
being blushed

A ship stops to
Wait for the sunset

If the ship catches the sunset
We will be in eternity

"If the ship sails into the sun
It will enter a beautiful
And brand new world"

"You will pull me to run to it"
"I shall pick a flower for you"

But we are watching

The sunset is crunched, swallowed

By the clouds on the sea.

2021/9/22

2022 Formosa Poetry Festival

Poets in the screen

Are reading poems aloud

Poets sitting in chairs

Think of, sometimes look back

The collected poems on display stands

They chant in heart

The plague still chases after time flow

And chases human being

Who will be the next one, caught by the plague?

Now who is chanting poems?

Oh! again and again

After the library is shut down

The plague cannot catch poems

2022/9/20

At the library of Tamkang Univ.

Sunset Glow

Is it a sunset glow or colored ribbon?
Slowly drifting in wind to the tower
    Which looks like a spotlessly white palace
Is it coming to find her?

However, it is not sure
Where to drop

Is it possible that
she hides herself
in the green grasses on the hill
and smiles, looking the ribbon

2022/9/19

167

Water Drops

As steel balls

Water drops one after another fall to

The golden pond in

afterglow

Why makes no splashed water

Why do drops not sink

Oops! They fall on

The sunset clouds in sky

2022/9/21

Climber on the Top

The sunset clouds
Are going to disappear soon

That man who quickly walked to
The top of the trail
Needs to jump up
Then he can leap easily on
the sunset clouds

To accuse the daemons of making war
To invade peoples
And crazily want to
Enslave peoples

However, he gazes at the ground
And tries hard to hear clearly
What daemons promise him

Sunset clouds disappear

in the silent sigh

again as before

2022/9/23

Blooming Too Late

In Tamsui riverside
That poinciana
Is just recently blooming in
Red but sparse flowers

Alas! blooming is too late!
They are gazing Mt. Guanyin
And praying at all times

Late flowers are nothings!
What can they pray for?

A vast expanse of fog
becomes orange red suddenly

and flies to Mt. Guanyin

and jumps into Tamsui river

and runs to the late flowers by treading water

What those late flowers have done!

2022/9/20

Vines and Poems

Poems were written on pottery leaves
And pasted on the slope of
Country road in Churyo
The leaves won't be withered

Someone walks in the road
And reads the poems softly

Ah! Vines
Climb onto pottery leaves
Reading and holding poems

"I want not to be withered
I want to become a pottery leaf"

Will the poet who wrote the poem
Be immortal and ever-young?

2022/10/12

Robbing the Spring

Whom does Spring belong to?

Tanks of Russia
Invaded Ukraine
Crushing spring fields
To rob the spring of Ukraine

That man, rubbing his eyes
Gazes, and observes
To find out how to invade
And rob the spring of Taiwan

I am walking by the spring fields
The aquatic birds are bowing to peck
Suddenly they flee about
And splash rows of water
Are they frolicking
or driving out each other?

Just after a moment, they stop
When they are
far away from each other
Which aquatic bird can
snatch and monopolize spring?

2023/2/26

Chickens

My students ask me

Why does that man shout so loudly

he wants to go to China to make

sacrifices to his ancestors

"Does he return hometown with jewels and honors?"

"Does he retire to return hometown in dream?"

They quarrel violently

I cough slightly to say

When I was a child

my parents herded a few chickens

Firstly, I strongly hated they asked me

To call chickens back to the poultry house

They ran around so wildly

I didn't know which chicken I should chase

Once, I saw the lady next door
Pursed her lips to call, "zhu ~ zhu!"
One by one, chickens rushed out to her
Pecking the grains of rice, they walked
into the poultry house

"Did your chickens also run to her?"

"No! no! only her chickens
She called them so to feed them everyday"

Even she called in the same way
When she wanted to kill one to eat
The chickens also ran
and flied back to her

"Sir! Is this a fable story?"

"Could it be said that

That man is a Chinese chicken?"

"Ah, chickens are livestock!"

Once again students quarrel and din

2023/3/21

Love is Beautiful

Love is beautiful as
Dew drops on the petals

But when did flowers fad and fall
And dews drop to vanish in the ground?

Oh! A flower is blooming again

Where does it come from?

2023/3/28

Forever

In a newly built
crescent gate, made of bricks
they hold each other's hands
What are they looking at?
murmuring about forever

The crescent moon enters
the gate once more
to find that pair of lovers
But only me, the irrelevant one

I softly touch
the bricks of centenary goalposts
Suddenly, who tenderly
whispers to me?
"Didn't you say forever?"

2023/9/21
At Tamsui Red Castle

The End

I can't help but
Leaving the crowd in a hurry
To look for the sunset

Would I eagerly ask again?
Why do you want the sunset
Explode and burn
To be scattered in the air

No! I am only surprised
That I am no longer agitated
That's all
What I have been given

Who is sighing behind me?
She is staring at me
Eyes like stars

And walking towards me
But suddenly I don't know
Where she is

"You haven't found yourself
that I have made you yet"

2023/9/23

One-century Tiles

Do not touch the tiles

Time is caught by them

It will escape and pull you go

2023/9/23
At Tamsui churyo

The Images
of Sun Through Leaves

Under the tree in early fall
She is an image of sun through a leaf
Light and agile as breezes

She and an image of sun
embrace each other to dance
That image suddenly condenses
To be a fallen leaf

She circles the fallen leaf
To turn it
And continuously murmurs
"Why did you hide yourself
Under a fallen leaf ?"

The fallen leaf has been blown away by winds

Where does the image under the leaf

Going?

2023/9/25

Poems With Sunshine

What makes them trapped?

They can't come here

On the revetment of the creek

Along the curved country road in Churyo

How were their poems written

on pottery leaves

which were taro leaves originally?

If they were here

And read out their poems

The curse of plagues and wars will be

Hails, melting in sunshine

In dappled sunshine,

I walk along the curved lane

Finally

I find their poems

Who are reading aloud their poems?
They look back and smile
Poems are running, jumping
and carrying sunshine to us

No more plague and war
forever

2023/10/8

Grasses in The Wind

Two grasses are about to hold hands with each other
But suddenly blown away by the wind

Once again, they
Approach each other in the wind
What do they eager to say?

What happened to the wind?
It blows them away again

Two lovers are busy in
Pushing these two grasses closer
The wind by passes
their palms again and again
to separate the grasses

The wind is getting stronger

They are suddenly blown to be apart

And sit on the grass

They hold hands tightly

At a loss like two grasses

2023/10/31

The Yellow Scarf

Is here breeze or not
Under green trees, is she
wearing a yellow scarf?
Is she coming closer?

I, still a teenager,
holding the poem I just wrote
staring at her
go forward and back

She brushes her hair
and floating silk scarves away
She looks at me
The silk scarf is suddenly blown away by the wind

I chase her scarf
Dark yellow leaves

all fly towards me

Suddenly I am an old man

She's gone

Where does the scarf float to?

Chasing the laughter

Boys and girls run out from the school gate

2023/10/31

Pink Poui Trees

In dust haze

Pink Poui trees are joyful on cloud

To be blooming all of a sudden

But suddenly

the flowers fall and scatter

Oy! Such a world!

It is better to die young

But why do they in a hurry

grow dense green leaves?

Are they looking forward to next year?

2024/3/23

A Firefly

I.

When it was getting dark, he watched
Plastic bowls, bags, bottles and jars scattered
In the water flowing through his land
"Once it is converted into construction land,
I would sell it" he talked to himself

A firefly was flying by the water
Flashing and flying towards him
Going back and forth around him
He followed it curiously

He saw an old man and a lady
Struggling to pick up trash from the water

The lady tried to pick up two loads of garbage

He hurriedly picked them up for her

She tilted her head and smiled

Looking at him panting

That firefly lighted her eyes up

II.

After they went back and forth several times

Where did fireflies fly out from?

Like non-stop fireworks

Was it a stream or a river of fireflies?

It is hard to distinguish

She laughed like little bells
"Grandpa! It's done!"
The old man turned around and bowed to him
Suddenly jumped into the stream of blinking light
He screamed and rushed at the old man
She ran to him and held him

The old man emerged from the dancing light spots
He stood up and became a child
He waved to us, looking back again and again
finally walked away

She said slowly, "Thank you! Grandpa is reborn"

III.

"Then, what about the lady ?"

He takes a long sigh, "I regain the land
Remove garbage and use no pesticides or chemical fertilizers
Only use what the earth gives."

"Wow! So long and wide
The flowing and rippling river of fireflies!"

He wandered silently by the river of fireflies
Whom is he looking for?

2024/4/22

About the Author

Ming-Keh Chen. He received a PhD in physics from Nat'l Tsing Hua University in 1986, and in 2023 he retired from the Department of Physics, Nat'l Chung-Hsing University as a professor.

He is a member and social affairs committee member of Li poetry society. His publication includes twelve collected poems, and two collected short stories. He was awarded night prizes of literature in Taiwan.

語言文學類　PG3050　台灣詩叢22

詩帶著陽光
Poems With Sunshine
——陳明克漢英雙語詩集

作　　者 / 陳明克（Chen Ming-Keh）
責任編輯 / 吳霽恆
圖文排版 / 許絜瑀
封面設計 / 張家碩

發 行 人 / 宋政坤
法律顧問 / 毛國樑　律師
出版發行 / 秀威資訊科技股份有限公司
　　　　　114台北市內湖區瑞光路76巷65號1樓
　　　　　電話：+886-2-2796-3638　傳真：+886-2-2796-1377
　　　　　http://www.showwe.com.tw
劃撥帳號 / 19563868　戶名：秀威資訊科技股份有限公司
　　　　　讀者服務信箱：service@showwe.com.tw
展售門市 / 國家書店（松江門市）
　　　　　104台北市中山區松江路209號1樓
　　　　　電話：+886-2-2518-0207　傳真：+886-2-2518-0778
網路訂購 / 秀威網路書店：https://store.showwe.tw
　　　　　國家網路書店：https://www.govbooks.com.tw

2024年7月　BOD一版
定價：280元
版權所有　翻印必究
本書如有缺頁、破損或裝訂錯誤，請寄回更換

讀者回函卡

國家圖書館出版品預行編目

詩帶著陽光：陳明克漢英雙語詩集 = Poems with sunshine/
陳明克著. -- 一版. -- 臺北市：秀威資訊科技股份有限
公司, 2024.07
　　面；　公分. -- (語言文學類 ; PG3050)(台灣詩叢 ; 22)
中英對照
BOD版
ISBN 978-626-7346-95-2(平裝)

863.51　　　　　　　　　　　　　　　113008646